WHEN THE JURY COMES BLACK

A Novella By
ZULU ALI, ESQ.

Published by 10 Nubian Queens & 5 Kings Media

DEDICATION

Dedicated to My First and Only Love -
My Soulmate and wife Charito Ali

ABOUT THE AUTHOR

Zulu Ali is a practicing **trial attorney, social entrepreneur, social commentator, and activist**. A former police officer and U.S. Marine Corps veteran, he earned a juris doctorate in law (J.D.) from Trinity International University Law School; a masters in administration of justice (M.S.) and business (M.B.A.) from University of Phoenix; an undergraduate degree with a focus on African studies from Regents College through a consortium with Tennessee State University; and is a doctoral scholar researching pan-African social entrepreneurship at California Southern University.

Attorney Ali is the founder and principal attorney at the Law Offices of Zulu Ali and Associates, LLP based in Riverside, California (zulualilaw.com), which is the largest Black-owned law firm in California's Inland Empire. The firm focuses on representing persons accused of crimes, immigrants, and persons seeking civil justice in state and federal courts. Ali is counsel at the African Court of Justice and Human Rights in Tanzania and the International Criminal Court at The Hague, Netherlands. Attorney Ali and his law firm take on extremely difficult cases and matters that provide an opportunity to make changes in the law, through the courts, when the law is unjust.

Attorney Ali served as Director of the American Committee for United Nations Oversight, an advocacy group that lobbied the United Nations for police reform in 2015. He is the Director of the Stop and Frisk Youth Leadership Academy, which mentors and trains at-risk youth to deal with police encounters; Director of the Southern California Veterans Legal Clinic, a legal clinic offering no cost and low cost legal services to military veterans; and a member of Iota Phi Theta Fraternity, Inc. serving on the international governing body (Grand Council) as General Legal Counsel.

In 2017, Attorney Ali was recognized as one of the most influential African American Leaders in Los Angeles by the National Action Network founded by Reverend Al Sharpton. In 2022, Attorney Ali, along with his daughter Attorney Whitney Ali, were recognized as s two of the Most Influential People of African Descent (MIPAD), Law and Justice Edition. MIPAD is a global civil society initiative in support of the International Decade for People of African Descent, proclaimed by United Nation's General Assembly resolution 68/237.

Attorney Ali has been Honored as a Top Lawyer by the National Black Lawyers-Top 100 and National Trial Lawyers-Top 100; a Top 10 Lawyer by the American Academy of Trial Attorneys, American Institute of Legal Counsel, American Jurist Institute, and Attorney & Practice Magazine; Rue Ratings Best Lawyer in America. Ali has been inducted into Marquis Who's Who Biographical registry for excellence in law and activism and received the Albert Neilson Marquis Lifetime Achievement Award.

He is the founder and CEO of 10 Nubian Queens & 5 Kings Media (http://10nubianmedia.com), a mass media production company focusing on black family and social justice content in film, radio, theater, music, and book publishing.

Ali produced the documentary film *Purpose & Freedom: Keep Your Hand on the Plow*, which premiered at the Wilshire Screening Room in Beverly Hills in 2017 and on-demand (purposeand-freedommovie.com); wrote and produced the stage play *Purpose & Freedom: The Story of Attorney Zulu Ali & Aracely Morales*, which premiered at the Hudson Theater in Hollywood in January 2020; wrote, produced, and is featured in the doculecture film *Negros For Sale: The Business of American Criminal Justice* to be released in December 2020; and wrote and produced a musical compilation with various artists titled The Discography of Zulu Ali (2020) (https://zulualimusic.hearnow.com).

Attorney Ali authored the books *Interview with a Black Lawyer Fighting for Justice* (2020); *When the Jury, Money, Votes, and Pride Comes Black (2020)*; *Lecture on Black America and American Justice: A History & Paradigm of Retributive Psychosis* (2016); and *Black Man's Religion: Islam or Christianity* (1997), a copy of which is in the Collection of Rosa Parks Papers at the Library of Congress.

Attorney Ali co-founded the Nubian Royalty Kids Book Series, which publishes animated books to educate children on subjects that impact and empower the black and minority community. As part of the series, Ali has written the children's books *Izem Meets Officer Joe: Izem Learns to Deal with Police Encounters* released in November 2020; and *Amayah & Tye's Lemonade Stand: A Lesson on Building Community Wealth*, to be released in December 2020.

Additionally, Zulu Ali is host of the podcast and radio talk show Justice Watch with Attorney Zulu Ali (justicewatchradio.com) which broadcasts from NBC Radio studio in Redlands, California; and he is a member of the National Black Radio Hall of Fame (Chicago chapter).

Ali has been married to his wife (Charito) since 1986, they have four adult children (Christine, Whitney, Ashley, and Lynda), five grandchildren (Amayah, Tye, Izem, Amina, and Nasira), and resides in Southern California with his family.

INDEX

PROLOGUE

The city street buzzed with life as the trio—Sarah, Marcus, and Jamal—made their way down the sidewalk. The sun hung low, casting long shadows that stretched across the pavement, and the air was thick with the sounds of traffic and the chatter of pedestrians. Their conversation was intense, fueled by the events that had unfolded just moments ago on the corner of the street. A black man and a white woman had clashed in a heated exchange, their voices rising in anger as a small crowd gathered to watch.

"I still can't believe what we just witnessed," Sarah said, her voice trembling with emotion.

She was a tall woman with fiery red hair, her eyes flashing with a mix of frustration and sadness beneath the brim of her baseball cap. Marcus, a young man with a rugged charm and a determined set to his jaw, nodded in agreement.

"It's like a punch to the gut, seeing that kind of hatred out in the open," he said, his voice tight with anger.

Jamal walked beside them, his expression grave. His dark skin seemed to absorb the harsh light of the setting sun, giving him an air of quiet intensity.

"It's a reminder of the reality we're living in," he said, his voice low but firm.

"A reality where black lives are still seen as disposable."

They walked in silence for a moment, the weight of their words hanging heavy in the air. Then, Sarah spoke up again, her voice filled with determination.

"But we can't let ourselves be paralyzed by despair," she said, her fists clenched at her sides. "We have to use our voices, our actions, to fight against this injustice."

Marcus nodded, his gaze focused on the path ahead.

"You're right," he said, his voice steady. "We can't afford to stay silent. We have to speak out, to stand up for what's right."

Jamal's eyes flashed with a fierce resolve as he looked at his friends.

"And we can't just fight against individual acts of racism," he said, his voice rising with passion. "We have to confront the systems that perpetuate it. The institutions that uphold white supremacy."

They walked on, their footsteps echoing against the pavement, each lost in their own thoughts. But despite the heaviness of their conversation, there was a sense of solidarity between them, a shared commitment to making a difference. As they rounded the corner, they came face to face with a mural that adorned the side of a nearby building. It depicted the faces of activists, both past and present, their eyes filled with determination and defiance. Sarah stopped in front of the mural, her eyes tracing the contours of each face.

"Look at them," she said, her voice filled with awe. "They fought against impossible odds, but they never gave up. They never stopped fighting for what they believed in."

Marcus nodded, his gaze lingering on the mural.

"They inspire us to keep pushing forward, no matter how daunting the challenge may seem," he said, his voice filled with determination.

Jamal reached out and placed a hand on Sarah's shoulder, his touch gentle but reassuring.

"We may not have all the answers," he said, his voice calm. "But as long as we stand together, we can overcome anything."

And with that, they continued on their journey, their hearts filled with hope and their minds set on creating a better future for all. For in the face of adversity, they knew that their voices were powerful, their actions meaningful. And as they walked, side by side, they knew that they were not alone. As they walked, the city seemed to pulsate with the rhythm of their conversation, the vibrant energy of the streets echoing their passion for change.

People passed by, their faces a blur of indifference or curiosity, but the trio remained focused on their mission. Sarah's gaze drifted from the mural to the bustling city around them, her thoughts swirling with a mix of determination and doubt.

"Sometimes I wonder if our efforts even make a difference," she confessed, her voice tinged with uncertainty.

Marcus glanced at her, his expression sympathetic.

"I know it can feel overwhelming at times," he said, his voice soft. "But every small action we take, every conversation we have, it all adds up. We may not see the results right away, but we have to believe that change is possible."

Jamal nodded in agreement, his eyes reflecting the flickering lights of the storefronts they passed.

"And we can't underestimate the power of community," he said, his voice growing stronger. "When we come together, united in our commitment to justice, we become unstoppable."

They walked on, their footsteps falling in sync with the beat of their collective determination. The city seemed to fade into the background as they delved deeper into their conversation, exploring the complexities of race, privilege, and oppression. Sarah spoke of her own experiences with discrimination, her voice trembling with raw emotion as she recounted the countless times she had been judged based on the colour of her skin.

Marcus shared stories of his upbringing in a predominantly white neighbourhood, where he had felt like an outsider, never fully accepted for who he was. Jamal spoke of the systemic barriers he had faced throughout his life, barriers that threatened to derail his dreams before they had even begun. But amidst the pain and frustration, there was also a sense of hope, a belief that their struggles were not in vain. They spoke of the progress that had been made, however slow and incremental it may have been, and the countless individuals who had paved the way for future generations to thrive. As they approached the end of the street, their conversation began to taper off, the weight of their words hanging heavy in the air. But their resolve remained unwavering, their commitment to justice stronger than ever.

"We may not have all the answers," Sarah said, her voice filled with determination. "But as long as we continue to speak out, to stand up for what's right, we can't be silenced."

Marcus nodded, a fierce determination burning in his eyes.

"And we won't stop fighting until every voice is heard until every life is valued and respected."

Jamal smiled, a sense of quiet satisfaction spreading across his face.

"Together, we can create a future where justice prevails," he said, his voice ringing with certainty.

And with that, they walked on into the gathering dusk, their footsteps echoing against the pavement, their hearts filled with hope for a better tomorrow. For as long as they had each other, they knew that anything was possible.

CHAPTER 1

Myron Peterson, who was nineteen years old, a black athletic build male, walked up to an apartment door and knocked. He had a backpack strung over one shoulder. He rocked back and forth nervously. The door opened. Amanda York, who was nineteen, a white female stood at the door in a white T-shirt and grey sweatpants. Her long blonde hair was tied in a ponytail.

Amanda York, "Hey." Myron, "Hey."

She stepped back so he could enter. She closed the door behind him.

7 WEEKS LATER

Inside the jury room, there was a long conference table in the middle of the room with five chairs on one side of the table, four on the other and one at each end. There were two windows with a view to the main street and filled bookcases on every wall.

The door opened and a Deputy, Marty Stewart, who was in his late 20s, a white male, walked in and held the door open. Another Deputy, Anthony Johnson, a 50 year old black male walked and stood against the wall beside Marty. A group of people begin to enter in a single file line. Charles Hood, a seventy-five years old black male, in good physical shape for a man his age with a head full of grey hair, walked in first and immediately went towards one of the chairs at the head of the table.

Emily Washington, a 40 years old white female, with long black hair, dressed business casual, walked in next. She helped Charles into his seat and sat in a chair next to him.

Jorge Rodriguez, a Mexican male in his late 40s, who was wearing a clean mechanic's shirt that had his name on it, walked in and found a seat. Soo Lee, a Korean female in her mid-30s walked into the room wearing a long-sleeved, black collarless shirt. Her gold cross hanging from a necklace around her neck. She found a seat.

Trevor "Malik" Banks, a twenty-eight-year-old black male, walked in wearing a jacket that was zipped up all the way to his neck. He found a seat and sat down. He rushed to unzip the jacket and took it off, revealing a Kinte cloth print shirt with Black Lives Matter in white print across the front. He tried to hand Deputy Johnson the jacket.

Deputy Johnson said, "Nah, you hold on to that. You heard what the judge said. If she sees that shirt again she's going to hold you in contempt of court."

Deputy Stewart shook his head. "What were you thinking?"

Deputy Johnson gave Deputy Stewart an admonishing look.

Stewart, "What?"

Trevor, "Just in case the court needed a reminder." Mercedes Shepard, a twenty years old black female, who was wearing a USC tee shirt, walked in and heard Trevor's comment.

Mercedes said, "A reminder of what, that you don't have any respect for the courtroom?"

Trevor pointed to the shirt.

"Why is this disrespectful? Is it a lie?" Mercedes wasn't happy at all.

Mercedes, "You're lucky she didn't throw your ass out the courtroom."

Trevor said, "Oh I bet she wanted to. They're already oppressing one brother why not get a two-for-one."

"Oh brother..." Trevor was sarcastic. "Oh, sister..." He said.

Deputy Johnson interrupted between them.

Deputy Johnson, "Enough. Keep it down until I give you these instructions."

Mercedes sat as far away from Trevor as possible and they glared at each other. Deputy Johnson looked around for a moment.

On the other side, Jesse Ward, a forty-year-old black male, walked in shaking his head at Mercedes and Trevor. Sanayah Bukhari, a Pakistani female in her mid-30s, who was dressed formally, walked in wary, paying close attention to where everyone was sitting before she decided to pick a seat next to Mercedes.

Brad Kennedy, a thirty-year-old white male, was wearing slacks and a blazer over a white button-up shirt. He was wearing a red baseball cap as he walked through the door.

Johnson, "Hat." Brad looked at him.

Brad, "What? We're not in the..."

Before he could say more, Deputy Johnson interrupted his sentence.

Johnson said, "...you're still in the courthouse, remove your hat sir."

Brad looked over at Deputy Stewart. He was very confused, but he knew he had to do it. Deputy Stewart looked at Deputy Johnson, then back at Brad and shrugged.

Stewart, "You heard him."

Brad Kennedy snatched the hat off his head and looked for a seat. He shook his head.

Brad says, "Every day it's like another right is snatched away from us."

Again, Trevor broke the silence. Trevor said, "Give me a break."

Johnson looked at him as he got a bit frustrated by Trevor.

Johnson, "Don't start."

Trevor raised his hands in deference. Ahmed Badawi, a fifty-year-old Palestinian, male, wearing a sweater and khakis and eyeglasses, walked in observing everyone's location and demeanour before he chose a seat.

David Goldberg, a Jewish male in his mid-40s, wearing a short button-up shirt, untucked, with jeans, walked towards the last chair.

Gladys Cook, a sixty years old black, female, with beautiful skin, no make-up, with shoulder-length salt and pepper, mostly salt hair, walked slowly into the room. David saw her and realized there weren't any more chairs. He stopped before he sat down and pulled the chair out for Gladys.

Gladys Cook said, "Thank you, sweety." David smiled a bit and nodded.

David Goldberg said, "No problem." Then he looked at Deputy Stewart. "We need another chair."

Deputy Stewart nodded and looked at Johnson. Then he said. "You got this?"

Johnson, "Yeah, go ahead."

Deputy Stewart walked out, letting the door close behind him.

Johnson, "All right ladies and gentlemen. Remember your instructions from the judge. Engage in open and respectful dialogue. Everybody in here is entitled to their opinion."

Something which had made Brad more confused as again he interrupted in between Johnson's sentence.

Brad said, "That's what makes this country so great."

Johnson wasn't happy about this as he looked at Brad and replied.

Johnson said, "Excuse me, Mr. Kennedy, I'm talking."

"My fault, continue."

Johnson nodded and looked around for a moment.

Then again, he began to speak.

"The deliberation process cannot work unless you all respect the views of your fellow jurors."

This time each one of them was listening to him carefully.

"Weigh the evidence, consider the testimony of the witnesses and their credibility and consider any possible reasonable doubt," Johnson added.

The deputy walked back into the room carrying another chair and handed it to David Goldberg.

Stewart said, "There you go." David nodded.

David said, "Thanks."

Deputy Johnson, "All right folks, we'll be right outside this door.

Everyone nodded.

"If you need anything, just knock." He said.

After completing his lines, he nodded in agreement and then looked at Stewart.

"C'mon…"

Deputy Johnson and Stewart walked out and closed the door behind them. The room got quiet as everyone was silent.

CHAPTER 2

All the jurors were sitting at the table and were uncomfortable. Some were looking at each other, while others avoided eye contact. Soo Lee broke the silence of the room.

Soo Lee says, "So how do we start?"

Again, Brad interrupted as he was in a hurry or curious about something.

Brad, "Start what? This is an open and shut case." Everyone looked at him.

"He did it. Let's go home."

Trevor was confused by his words. Trevor, "Open and shut?"

Brad said, "That's right."

On the other side, Sanayah Bukhari broke her silence.

Sanayah Bukhari says, "I agree." Trevor says, "Of course you do."

Mercedes also jumped in between. Mercedes, "Leave her alone."

"What does that mean, "of course you do?"" Sanayah Bukhari.

"Ignore him," Mercedes said.

Emily Washington asked, "I'm sorry but um, what makes you think this case is so open and shut?"

Brad said, "Uh, everything. You were in the same courtroom I was in sweety..."

Emily wasn't happy with his lines.

Emily Washington said, "Don't call me sweety." Brad said, "You heard the evidence."

Emily was confused.

"You heard the girl's testimony," Brad added.

Emily Washington says, "What evidence? There was none."

Trevor interrupted in between them.

Trevor, "Except for the white girl's testimony." Everyone looked at him.

"The same white girl that waited four weeks to report the alleged rape. Come on man."

Sanayah replied. "Perhaps she was afraid." Trevor shook his head.

Trevor said, "Perhaps she was getting her lie straight.

Her little white lie."

Mercedes, "Oh will you give it a rest?" Trevor was annoyed.

"Oh, I got it now. You're one of those. You done forgot what team you play for. Well, take a look in the mirror girl."

Mercedes was silent, but Trevor was furious.

"I'll give you one good reason why they'll never welcome you to that side with open arms, no matter how many times you hate on your own people." He said.

She rolled her eyes and flipped him the bird. David tried to handle the argument because he understood where it was getting.

David said, "Okay, okay, look everyone, let's not turn this into a race thing, okay?"

All of the black people in the room stopped and turned towards David in disbelief. Brad laughed.

"Come on now." He said. Trevor looked at him.

Brad, "You know nothing bad can happen to one of them in this country without somebody playing the race card."

This line also made Jesse a bit furious and questionable.

"One of them? Who are you talking about when you say, "them?"" Jesse Ward.

Brad and Jesse glared at each other. Brad smirked.

David said, "Okay, okay, everybody, let's not get too far ahead of ourselves. Remember what the judge said, we need to pick a foreman first thing."

Everyone looked at him and nodded in agreement.

"So, does anyone want to volunteer to be the foreman?"

The room was silent. Brad said, "Well hell..." "Hell no," Trevor said.

Some of them tried to muffle their giggles. David said, "Anyone else?"

They all looked around the room at each other without speaking.

Charles Hood, "Guess the job is yours, son." David shook his head.

David, "Mine? Oh no, I wasn't volunteering."

"Yeah, you did. When you shut those two up. You got the ball rolling, might as well stick with it." Charles said.

David looked at everyone. No one had objected. Trevor shrugged his shoulders. He paused for a moment.

"Well, okay then. So, what I think we should do first is…" David said.

Emily was the first one to answer.

Emily Washington said, "The first thing you want to do is take a vote. Find out where everyone is on the verdict. Then, depending on the results, we start to deliberate."

David nodded.

"Discuss what little evidence was presented, theories, credibility, all of the things the judge told us to consider." She said.

Gladys Cook says, "You sound like you've done this before."

Emily said, "Not exactly."

Ahmed Badawi interrupted for the time. Ahmed, "Then what exactly?"

Emily smiled with confidence.

Emily said, "I'm a retired Florida District Attorney."

Trevor said, "Oh, then we know what your vote is don't we."

Emily was stern.

"You don't know anything about me."

Mercedes, "You're off to a great start making friends."

Trevor smiled.

He said, "I got enough friends."

Again, David tried to handle the moment.

"Okay guys, please. You heard her. Let's take a vote.

So, everyone who thinks…" David said.

Jorge, "You want to just say it out in the open for everyone to see?"

"What you got to be afraid of Papi'?"

Jorge looked at him with confusion on his face. As Brad added.

"I saw the way you were looking at that boy. You know he's guilty." He said.

Jorge, "I did not say that. I…" Trevor, "Boy?"

Brad, "Oh here we go. The kid is 19 years old, what am I supposed to call him, a man? Men don't rape innocent little girls."

Ahmed Badawi said, "How do you know she is such an innocent little girl?'

Trevor says, "You know why he thinks that." Brad looked at him.

"Give me a break, would ya?"

Emily looked at David as she was waiting for him to intervene.

David, "Uh okay, fellas, let's cam down. Stay focused okay."

Again, everyone looked at him.

"A man's freedom is in our hands. So, it's okay, we can do an anonymous vote. Some of the jurors moan in disagreement."

Jesse said, "What's the point of hiding our votes if we have to sit in here and try to change each other's minds anyway? Might as well do it out in the open and get right to it."

David, "Okay then, everybody okay with a simple show of hands?"

The jurors looked at each other and then they all nodded.

"Fine. In that case, if you think the defendant is guilty raise your hand." David says.

Brad Kennedy's hand quickly shot up first. Next, Mercedes Shepard raised her hand.

Trevor shook his head in disappointment. "Why am I not surprised?" He said.

Mercedes says, "Go to hell."

Sanayah Bukhari raised her hand next, then Soo Lee. Next, David Goldberg slowly raised his hand, avoiding eye contact with Gladys.

"Okay…" David. Jorge, "Wait."

Jorge raised his hand.

Trevor said, "You people are crazy." Jesse looked at him.

"Hey, relax lil' brother."

Trevor had a great look of disappointment and frustration on his face.

Trevor says, "How can I relax…how can you relax while this young kid gets railroaded? I'm not just going to sit here and let that happen."

Brad said, "Oh yeah, what are you going to do about it? See, that's what I'm talking about. It's like any time one of you gets into trouble, it's somebody else's fault."

Trevor shook his head.

"Never the knucklehead that committed the crime. But the cop that arrested him, or the judge that sentenced him, or God forbid…the victim. How about some accountability for once." Brad.

Trevor said, "Accountability? That's funny coming from you."

Brad, "You don't know me."

Trevor, "I know you're a privileged, entitled, white man, who refuses to take accountability for the systemic racism that you benefit from every day of your life."

Brad, "Here we go."

Gladys interrupted in between them.

Gladys, "Hey, stop it, both of you. We're here to do a job, not debate race in this country."

Trevor questioned, "Why not?"

Mercedes replied to him before anyone could.

She said, "Because it has nothing to do with this case."

"It has everything to do with this case!" Trevor.

Suddenly, the door opened and Deputy Stewart came in.

Stewart asked, "Everything okay in here?"

Trevor looked out the window frustrated. Deputy Stewart stared at him. "I said…" Stewart.

Charles, "Uh, yup, yes sir everything is fine. Just getting to know each other a little bit."

Deputy Stewart didn't believe it. He continued looking in Trevor's direction before finally backing out of the room.

"Okay then. Try to keep it down." Stewart. David says, "We will, sorry about that deputy."

Deputy Stewart closed the door. There was an awkward silence for a moment.

David, "Listen, I know this is a sensitive situation but we owe it to Ms. York…"

Ahmed, "And the boy."

David says, "Yes, of course, we owe it to them both to get this right."

He thought for a moment.

"So, since we're split right down the middle, I guess we'd better just start from scratch. Does anyone want to explain why they voted the way they did?" David said.

They all looked around the room waiting. Then Soo Lee said.

Soo Lee says, "My family owns a store in South Central and…"

Trevor, "Here we go." "Where at?" Jesse Ward.

Soo Lee, "Why does it matter?" Trevor replied before Jesse.

"It matters if you're trying to make it relevant to why we're here." Trevor.

Without thinking for a moment, Soo Lee replied.

Soo Lee, "The corner of W99th and Main Street." Jesse Ward contemplated, "I know that store." Gladys interrupted him as Soo Lee wasn't completed. She said, "Let her finish…"

Soo Lee, "Thank you. Well, if you know that store, then you know that we get robbed almost once a week."

Trevor said, "Call the police." Mercedes was angry.

She said, "Do you ever shut up?"

Soo Lee, "We do call the police all the time. But by the time they get there, the…"

Jesse Ward, "The what?"

"The…people are gone. They get away. Then they come back the next day and do it again." Soo Lee.

Brad, "Sounds like your daddy needs to invest in some security. And I ain't talking about no cameras."

Soo Lee, "My father is a peaceful man. He doesn't want to hurt anyone."

Brad said, "Well good luck with that…"

Jesse says, "So what's your point?"

Soo Lee said, "My point is, every day, young black boys come in and sometimes they look like trouble."

CHAPTER 3

Some of the black people in the room shook their heads and took offence. David looked around the room as he knew Soo Lee said something which he shouldn't have. Soo Lee also realized and immediately added to his words.

Soo Lee said, "But sometimes they look like good, clean boys."

He sighed as he covered his words. But Jesse had some other plans.

Jesse, "Clean?"

Soo Lee looked at him and answered his question "Clean, no trouble, smart, come from school. But they all steal from us."

Charles, "I'm still waiting for the point here."

"My point is that appearance doesn't make someone innocent or guilty. Mr. Peterson looks like a good student, a nice boy, but that doesn't show us what's on the inside." Soo Lee.

Her words made everyone around the room as she added more to it.

"Maybe he was angry, maybe he had a bad day and took it out on Ms. York."

Emily said, "The problem with that theory is that she never said any of that. There's no reason to believe that when he arrived at her apartment, he was in an altered state or emotional or anything. She didn't say any of that."

Soo Lee says, "That doesn't mean it isn't true."

Emily, "No, but we can't prove it. And if we can't prove it to be true, we can't use it as an argument for or against."

Soo Lee sat back in her seat as she was disappointed a lot.

David said, "Who wants to…"

Jesse interrupted in between David's words.

Jesse says, "Hold on a minute. What's the name of your family's store?"

Soo Lee, "Why?"

Jesse Ward, "You brought it up. Now you don't want to tell us the name of the store?"

Trevor said, "What do you think we're going to do, rob it?"

Brad, "Maybe."

Jesse and Trevor glared at Brad. Brad shrugged. Brad, "You asked."

Finally, Soo Lee replied to their question.

Soo Lee says, "It is "Lee Korean Market and Goods.""

Jesse said, "Yeah, that's what I thought." Charles says, "What about it?"

Jesse, "My little thirteen-year-old nephew had to spend two nights in a juvenile detention centre because her family accused him of stealing from their store. And he's a good kid, never stole anything in his life!"

They all looked at Soo Lee.

Soo Lee says, "I don't know your nephew." Jesse shook his head.

"My family would not call the police on an innocent boy."

Jesse, "So you calling me a liar or you saying my nephew is a thief?"

"If he steals, he's a thief." Soo Lee said. Jesse Ward got a bit angry.

"What?!"

Soo Lee says, "Maybe he did steal, you don't know!"

Jesse said, "I do know! And I know he's in therapy now because of those two nights he spent in juvie. He was a fun, smart, lovable kid who didn't even like to go outside anymore. Thanks to you and your family."

Again, David interrupted in between them.

David said, "Okay, hey, guys, let's dial it back. We're getting off track again."

Jesse looked down as he was disappointed.

"This isn't about your nephew or your father's store.

This is about a rape."

Emily says, "An alleged rape…"

David looked at her for a moment, then added. He said, "An alleged rape…"

Emily sighed.

David said, "So, please…let's do what we were brought here to do."

He looked at Jesse and Soo Lee. They both simmered down. Then, Ahmed said what she had in her mind for a long.

Ahmed, "I have a question. Does no one find it peculiar that Ms. York waited four weeks to go to the police?"

Mercedes, "Have you ever been raped?"

Again, Trevor was annoyed by Merecedes's reply. Trevor, "Oh come on."

Brad, "Whoa…"

Mercedes, "No, I'm serious."

Trevor looked at her with the correct explanations of her lines.

"Have any of you ever been raped? I haven't. So I would never presume to know what was going through the mind of someone who has. Fear, confusion, anger, who knows."

Mercedes looked at Ahmed.

"Does that make the crime any less heinous because she waited four weeks to go to the police?"

Trevor, "The alleged crime." "You tell 'em, sister," Brad said. "You can go to hell too."

Brad held up his hands in a surrender gesture.

"Or, how about this? How about she was never going to report it because it didn't happen? But then she found out she was pregnant and "uh oh", what in the world will momma and daddy think if they find out their sweet little angel has been knocking boots with a black guy? Oh, I know…I'll say he raped me!" Trevor said.

"Oh my God." Mercedes.

"Sounds possible. It's not like it's never happened before." Jesse said.

Sanayah Bukhari, "Don't you think the police would be able to tell if she was lying? They're trained to…"

Trevor said, "Shoot unarmed black people?"

Sanayah, "To find the truth. They are trained to always find the truth."

Gladys, "Oh darling, you don't really believe that do you?"

"Of course, yes, I do. And you should as well. The police are here to protect us and help us." Sanayah.

"Naive much?" Trevor.

"They protect who they want to protect. And others…" Gladys.

She paused while speaking. Everyone waited patiently as she looked down at the table. She wiped a tear from her eye before it rolled down her face.

Emily, "Are you okay?"

Gladys nodded silently. She cleared her throat. "You're right, the police are supposed to protect citizens and keep us safe. But sometimes we need someone to protect us from the police. At least, people that look like us do."

She pointed to Trevor, Charles, Jesse and Mercedes. Gladys, "… and my son."

Ahmed, "Did something happen to your son?" Gladys, "He was killed."

She nodded.

"By a cop?" Trevor.

"I am sorry. I did not mean…" Ahmed.

Gladys, "It's okay. I just…I want her to hear this." Gladys looked at Sanayah.

"My Darnell, he…he was a little bit of a troublemaker. Not a bad boy, just impressionable…hung out with guys who he thought were his friends. But they weren't. Well, one night they talked him into breaking into some movie house in the hills and having a pool party. Of course, the police show up and…they say he fired first. I didn't even know he knew how to shoot a gun. So the police fired back. He was hit three times."

The room was in stun.

"The coroner said he was dead before his body hit the ground." She said.

More tears were rolling down her face. Mercedes grabbed a box of tissue from a table in the corner and handed the tissue to Gladys.

"Thank you." Gladys.

The room was silent for a moment. The majority of the people around the room could feel the pain and situation of Gladys.

Sanayah, "I am sorry. Very sorry. But...your son, he was breaking the law."

Charles, "So he deserved to die?"

Sanayah says, "No, no of course not. But if he had not been breaking the law, the police would not have been there. No one would have been in that situation."

Brad, "Bingo..."

"Yeah well my nephew wasn't breaking the law and her father and the cops still treated him like a criminal," Jesse says.

Soo Lee looked away.

Jorge said, "But you know, with all the gang violence and other crime going on in this city, how the hell are the cops supposed to know who the criminals are and who isn't?"

Trevor jumped in between.

Trevor says, "Criminals are the ones committing crimes."

Jorge says, "You know what I mean..." Trevor said, "No, I don't."

Jorge, "Too many gangs, too many drive-by shootings, kidnappings, beatings. So if the police have to be hard on everyone just to make sure they get the bad guys, I'm okay with that."

Jorge's reply made Jesse furious.

Jesse said, "Be "hard on everyone"? They killed her son. You're okay with that."

"That's not what I said!" Jorge says.

Brad said snarkily, "That's kinda of what you said." Jorge looked at him.

"Shut up pendejo."

Deputy Johnson and Deputy Stewart were sitting in chairs right outside the Jury Room door. They could easily hear the jurors' voices clearly through the door. Deputy Stewart stood up.

Johnson said, "No, no...let 'em be…"

Stewart nodded.

Stewart says, "Sounds like they're getting pretty riled up again."

Johnson said, "Let 'em. If we keep running in there every time they raise their voices we'll be here all week."

Stewart didn't say anything.

"It's going to take some butting heads to get a decision on this one." Johnson.

Stewart said, "You think? It seems like a no-brainer to me."

Deputy Johnson looked over at Deputy Stewart and shook his head.

Back to the Jury room, where Brad Kennedy was standing up and looking out the window.

Emily said, "What I think we all have to remember is that as jurors, we're supposed to set aside our personal beliefs and biases and just look at the facts of this case."

Trevor said, "What facts? Everything we heard in that courtroom was he said, she says. Her word against his and in those situations when she is white and he is black, we already know the outcome."

Again, Brad replied to him.

Brad said, "Here we go. You know, if you people have such a problem with the way things are run in this country…"

Emily said, "Don't say it…"

Brad said, "Why don't you just leave?"

Charles wasn't happy with Brad's reply as he answered.

He said, "Why should we leave?" Brad turned his face at him.

"We have just as much right to be here as you. None of our bloodlines started on this land. And I don't see any Indians in here and they're the only ones who can legitimately call this country home."

Mercedes, "Native Americans…"

Charles admonished her with his eyes. Mercedes realized that she said wrong.

Charles said, "Nobody never taught you not to correct your elders?"

She looked away in shame.

Brad said, "All I'm saying is that all I ever hear about is what this country is doing wrong, how unfair this country is, how terrible it treats people."

Ahmed, "It is true that America has one of the highest hate crime rates in the world. Combined with gun violence it is very unsettling for an immigrant to settle here."

Brad, "So I'll ask my question again, why don't you go somewhere else?"

Trevor, "You're an asshole."

Suddenly, David slams his fist down on the table, making a loud enough noise to demand everyone's attention.

David, "Enough! It's been a long three weeks and I know we're all ready to go home and get out of this courthouse. But that's not going to happen if we can't have a civil conversation and come to a decision about this case."

There was a pin-drop silence in the room.

"So, please! Let's stick to the facts." David said.

Trevor, "There's that word again. What facts are you talking about Mr. Foreman? Because I don't remember hearing any."

Mercedes, "She said she told him to stop." Emily replied to her.

"That's not a fact. Not without a witness to corroborate it."

Gladys, "Which there isn't."

Soo Lee, "So, how are we supposed to decide if we can't trust what either of them says because there were no witnesses? It is impossible."

Brad said, "It's not impossible." Soo Lee looked at him.

"Listen, even if what you all are saying is true and this is just a case of he said she said, then let's look at the likelihood of who is telling the truth. What seems more probable in this situation? What does she have to gain from getting involved with him and then lying about it?" He says.

"It's like we said earlier, maybe getting pregnant spooked her. She was scared about what her father would think." Jesse said.

Brad, "Oh so now the dad is racist? We don't even know the man. He never even testified. How can you make that assumption?"

Trevor, "How can you assume he isn't?"

Brad said, "Because every white person in America isn't racist!"

Trevor says, "I bet you don't think you're racist either do you?"

David said, "Gentlemen."

Mercedes, "Look, I'm not saying that some crimes aren't racially motivated or that some people aren't falsely accused just because of the colour of their skin. I just don't feel like this is one of those times."

Ahmed, "And what makes you say that?"

"I don't know, I just...I mean, she's my age. We have a lot of things in common. She's in college like I am, she's in a sorority, and she does a lot of community service. She just seems like a nice girl and I know nice girls make mistakes too, but this would be a blatant false accusation that would cost a man his freedom. She just doesn't seem like that kind of girl." Mercedes.

Trevor, "Because she's white?' Mercedes was irritated by this.

She said, "No, of course not because she's white! I just said..."

"You just said all the stuff you have in common with her but didn't once mention the one thing you don't have in common. Let me ask you a question...and be honest. If that were you in that courtroom crying rape, do you think these people in this room who are ready to throw the book at that young man, would be just as convinced of his guilt?" Trevor says.

"Why wouldn't they?" Mercedes.

Trevor looked around the room at the people who voted "guilty".

Sanayah, "Of course! Si.'" Soo Lee, "Yes!"

Jorge, "Si'…"

"I don't see why not. This is about who the defendant is, not the victim." David.

They turned to look at Brad. He shrugged his shoulders.

Brad said, "Why not?"

CHAPTER 4

Trevor rolled his eyes before turning back to Mercedes with a look of disbelief on his face. Then he said to her.

"If you believe that, I have a bridge for sale in New York City."

Mercedes, "Why are you so cynical?" Trevor, "Why aren't you more cynical?"

Mercedes, "Because not all white people, like not all black people, are bad."

Trevor shook his head.

He says, "I never said they were. But it's safer for people that look like me, to assume the worst."

Mercedes, "You must miss out on meeting a lot of good people like that."

"I bet I miss out on a lot of bad ones too."

"My father always says that the ones who are first to point fingers are the ones you have to watch the closest." Mercedes.

Trevor, "Oh yeah, what's your dad, a philosopher or something?"

"No, he's a cop."

Trevor became animated as he threw his arms in the air.

Trevor said, "Oh, there we go. It all makes sense now. I had you pegged all wrong. I thought you were just some sister who made it out of the hood to a big-time school like USC and intentionally forgot where you came from."

Mercedes was agitated by that.

"Turned up your nose at your people. But now that I know your dad was a cop, I see, you were born with that stick up your..."

Finally, when the situation looked going too far, again, David interrupted him to control his words.

David, "Hey!"

Trevor looked into Mercedes' eyes. Neither of them blink.

Soo Lee, "I have a question."

David looked at him.

"Why was he at her apartment?" Jesse replied immediately.

He said, "She invited him over." Sanayah, "To study."

Trevor, "On a weekend?" Mercedes, "It's a thing."

Jesse, "Yeah but why her apartment? Why not the library or a Starbucks?"

Jesse looked around the room at everyone's face in question.

"She must have felt really comfortable with him to invite him to her place, even if it was just to study." He added.

"She never said she didn't like him," Mercedes said. Charles smiled a bit and said to her.

"Like him enough to cook dinner and clean up the apartment."

"What does that mean?" Mercedes.

"It means, would you go all out like that for a guy you were just planning on studying with?" Trevor said.

Some of the women discreetly looked away or shook their heads in no.

Emily said, "I think we have to be careful again, not to make any comments that could be misconstrued as blaming the victim."

Trevor said, "The alleged victim." Emily nodded.

She said, "Right? The alleged victim." Trevor didn't say anything this time.

"Just because she cleaned up and cooked a meal does not mean she was anticipating a romantic evening with Mr. Peterson." Emily.

Gladys, "But when he testified, he said that he walked into the apartment and it smelled like she had been burning scented candles and there was soft music playing and the table was set for dinner for the two of them. I know I'm getting old but that sounds more like a date-date than a study-date to me."

Trevor nodded and supported her statement immediately.

Trevor, "Exactly…"

Brad said, "Maybe she's just a hospitable host. You're reaching…"

"We're reaching?"

Brad nodded in agreement.

"We're in here deliberating over a rape that there's no evidence ever happened. No physical evidence…" Trevor says.

Soo Lee said, "Because she did not have a rape exam completed by the police."

This was what Trevor was waiting for. Trevor, "Why not?"

Mercedes, "It was four weeks later. There probably wouldn't have been much physical evidence left."

Trevor, "So back to the question from earlier. Why'd she wait so long to go to the cops?"

David tried to calm things again.

He said, "And we already agreed that blaming the victim is not the right way to go here."

Trevor said, "Which victim are we talking about?"

David, "Despite what your prejudices are against the police and apparently, white people, the fact is that the police saw found enough merit in her accusations to move forward with rape charges. And that's the bottom line."

Trevor shook his head in disagreement.

"How we got to this point should be irrelevant. We are here now." David.

Emily said, "Well, legally that's not true. The "how" is always relevant. Arrests are made in this country all the time under false pretenses…"

Ahmed nodded and agreed with her.

"It is why there are such a staggering number of convictions overturned every year."

Brad says, "Or maybe so many convictions get overturned because of this bleeding heart, woke culture that has infested the country."

Brad's statement had always been controversial and had always troubled many. This time it did to Jesse, but he didn't resist.

Jesse says, "I'm so sick of white people using that word and twisting it up to suit your own bigoted needs. What you think is woke is really just common decency. You heard what the woman said, convictions are getting overturned because cops are arresting people of colour over a bunch of b.s. that doesn't stand up under scrutiny in court."

David said, "Even if that's the case, that isn't what we have here."

Gladys, "It sounds like exactly what we have here…"

Jorge, "The gang bangers that terrorize my neighbourhood know how to cover their tracks. They know what the police can and can't do, so they get away with a lot. So I don't care if the cops have to cross some lines or do something…"

Emily said, "Unethical?"

Jorge, "I was going to say, unorthodox. I don't care if they have to do something unorthodox to get those hoodlums off the streets. Whatever it takes."

Charles, "Attitudes like that is what got Trayvon Martin killed. George Floyd, Breonna Taylor, Elijah McClain, Fred Brown, Amir Johnson, Andrew Brown, Latoya James…"

As Charles rattled off names, the room got sombre. Gladys wiped her eyes. Trevor angrily looked out the window. Jesse glared at Brad.

"Daunte Wright, Frederick Holder…I can keep going." Charles.

Gladys, "Don't…"

Charles, "All of those people and a whole lot more were killed by cops who were doing something they thought was unorthodox but justified. And they were wrong. Just like the police who arrested this boy without a lick of evidence were wrong!"

Brad, "This is ridiculous, we're not getting anywhere…"

Brad stormed over to the door and banged on it. Brad said, "Hey!"

David said, "What are you doing?"

He banged on it again until it swung open. Deputy Johnson walked in with Deputy Stewart right behind him. He approached Brad.

Deputy, "Everything all right in here?"

Brad, "No. No, everything is not all right. We're in here spinning our tyres because we got a bunch of left- wing, woke, yahoos in here who would rather stick it to "the man" than send a guilty man to prison."

Johnson, "First of all, calm down and take a step back."

Deputy Johnson addressed the entire room.

Johnson says, "Remember people, you're not in here to prove whether he did it or not. You're just here to decide if the prosecution did its job and proved that he committed this crime beyond a reasonable doubt. There is some doubt present. Now, you all don't have to agree and you don't have to like each other, but what you do have to do is come to some kind of mutual understanding to present to the judge…"

Ahmed, "And what if we cannot come to such a mutual understanding?"

Emily said, "Hung jury."

Soo Lee, "What does that mean?"

Emily, "It means that the judge will have to declare a mistrial."

Sanayah, "And then?"

Emily said, "Either the case will be dismissed or the prosecution will retry the case if they see fit. But I can tell you from my experience, a case like this with such little evidence, if it resulted in a deadlock the first time, the chances are slim to none that they'd retry it."

Trevor, "Welp, there you go. Let's go home…" Mercedes, "What?!"

Brad, "Hell no!"

Trevor said, "You heard the woman. If we can't make a decision…which we can't, then it's a mistrial. After that, it's out of our hands."

Brad, "Oh you'd love that, wouldn't you? Why are you going to the mat for this guy so hard anyway? Is he one of your homeboys or something?"

Trevor, "What?"

Brad said, "Y'all play ball down at the park together and listen to rap music together calling each other ni…"

Before he could finish, Trevor rushed Brad but the deputies intervened and held Trevor back. Trevor and Brad were both trying to get at each other. Deputy Johnson pushed Brad up against a wall and pointed his finger in his face.

Johnson, "Stop! Now!"

Brad swatted Deputy Johnson's finger out of his face.

Johnson says, "Keep pushing me. I got no problem telling the judge I had to lock your ass up for contempt. None."

Trevor was still trying to push past Deputy Stewart so the Deputy twisted Trevor's arm behind his back and slammed him down on the table.

Gladys, "Hey!"

The jurors were all caught off guard and shocked by the violent act.

Johnson, "Hey! Stewart!"

Trevor continued to struggle but he had no leverage. Deputy Stewart had all of his own body weight on top of Trevor's back.

Stewart, "Calm down!"

Trevor, "Get off of me!" Stewart, "I said calm down!" Mercedes said to Trevor. "Stop moving."

Trevor looked and saw the fear in Mercedes and Gladys's eyes.

Jesse said, "Hey man, let him up!"

Charles, "Stop fighting Youngblood. Calm down." Deputy Johnson walked over and grabbed Deputy

Stewart by the shoulder.

Johnson says, "That's enough!"

Trevor started to calm down and Deputy Stewart slowly and carefully started to release him. When he let him go, Trevor stood up and faced Deputy Stewart. They stood face to face. Trevor was seething, his breathing was heavy and his fists clenched.

Stewart, "You got something to say?"

Jesse walked up slowly behind Trevor and tapped him on the arm.

"Come on young brother, go sit down," Jesse said.

Trevor doesn't move. "Come on." Jesse.

Finally, Trevor relaxed his fists and he backed away. Trevor sat down. Mercedes was looking at him with tears in her eyes. She looked away.

Johnson, "Listen to me because this is the last time I'm going to say it. That...will never happen again. Not on my watch. If you all can't be civil, never mind peaceful, then I'll send all of your asses home with a citation for obstructing justice. And yes, it goes on your official record."

The jurors looked at Emily and she nodded for confirmation.

Johnson said, "Violence of any kind whether it be physical, verbal or implied, is forbidden in this building and this room. Am I clear?"

They mumbled in response. Johnson, "I said, am I clear?!" Everyone says, "Yes…"

He turned and grabbed Deputy Stewart by the arm and pushed him towards the door. Once they left, he slammed the door closed behind them.

CHAPTER 5

Back to the outside of the Jury room, where Deputy Stewart was sitting in his chair. Then Johnson said.

Johnson says, "Stand up." Stewart got confused.

Stewart, "What?"

Johnson, "Stand your ass up right now."

Deputy Stewart reluctantly followed the command. "What the hell was that?"

Stewart said, "What the hell was what? The kid was out of control. He..."

Johnson, "From my perspective it looked like you were the one out of control. Since when do we put our hands on jurors?"

Stewart looked at him as he was surprised by his response.

"Oh, so I was just supposed to let him attack that guy?"

"No, but you could have handled it without losing your cool."

Stewart said, "Losing my cool?"

Stewart shook his head as he didn't expect this from Deputy Johnson.

"I did what I was trained to do."

Johnson didn't say anything but looked around for a moment.

"I stopped the situation from escalating. The little thug is lucky he didn't get it worse."

"Thug?"

"You know what I mean." Johnson replied, "Elaborate." "What?"

"What makes him a thug?"

Stewart said, "He's a troublemaker. He…" Johnson interrupted in his statement immediately.

He said, "The good ol' boy in there was just as riled up as the kid. I didn't see you roughing him up."

"You had him under control."

Deputy Johnson stood silently as he was looking at Deputy Stewart disapprovingly.

Stewart said, "Are you…are you really pissed right now? Wait a minute, are you trying to say I grabbed that kid because he's black?"

Deputy Johnson didn't respond. Again, Stewart shook his head in disappointment.

Stewart said, "You hear him in there causing all that trouble, drawing this process out, making it take longer than it has to be. There's no reason why they shouldn't have already made a decision. We should be on our way home to our wives by now A.J., you know that."

"And what decision do you think they should have come to already?"

"Are you serious?" "One hundred per cent."

"Don't tell me you think that kid is innocent," Stewarts said.

"You don't?" Johnson asked.

"Hell no! He raped that girl and…" He replied.

Deputy Johnson took a quick step towards Deputy Stewart.

Johnson whispered, "Keep your goddamn voice down."

Stewart too whispered in his response.

"Are you kidding me A.J.? Are you drinking the racism Kool-aid too?"

"What makes you so sure he did it?"

Stewart was trying his best to convince him but Johnson was thinking differently.

"Why would she lie?" "That's not an answer."

"Fine, you tell me why you think he's not guilty then."

"Where's the evidence? Why'd she wait so long to go to the police? Why didn't any neighbours hear any sounds of a struggle?"

"Maybe he was covering her mouth or something," Stewart said.

Johnson said, "She never said that."

"Maybe she forgot!" "Sshhh! Quiet."

Stewart whispered, "You're unbelievable." Johnson said, "Yeah, that makes two of us."

CHAPTER 6

Later inside the Jury Room, everyone was sitting silently. Some of them had moved away from the table and were sitting alone. The room was eerily calm while everyone was consumed by their thoughts. David was sitting on the edge of the table, tapping a pen against the table.

Mercedes, "Can you…" David, "Oh, yeah, sure, sorry." He stopped the tapping.

David said, "Just for the record, can we take another vote?"

"Another one? For what?" Gladys.

David said, "It's been a while since the last vote." She shrugged. Then David asked everyone. "Okay?"

They all mumbled under their breath or nodded half-heartedly.

David, "Okay, raise your hand if you think Peterson is guilty."

David raised his hand first this time. Brad, Sanayah, Jorge, Mercedes and Soo Lee all follow suit. Everyone counted the hands.

Trevor said, "There's ten seconds we'll never get back."

He rolled his eyes as he was disgusted. The guilty voters lowered their hands frustrated.

Sanayah, "Why has this been so difficult? This is my first time on jury duty. Is it always like this?"

Brad, "Nope. I've been on juries before and we reached a verdict in fifteen minutes. We finished deliberating before lunchtime and pretended to be still undecided so we could get one last lunch from the fancy seafood place down the street from the courthouse."

Jesse says, "Way to fulfil your civic duty." Brad said, "Hey we got the job done." Brad nodded.

Sanayah said, "What kind of case was it?"

Brad said, "An old guy shot a kid through his front door in the middle of the night. The kid didn't die but he lost his arm."

Sanayah, "Why would he do that?"

"Kid had been at a party and drinking real hard and thought he had driven to his girlfriend's house. He was on the front porch banging on the door for her to let him in but he was at this old man's house. His girlfriend lived two blocks away." Brad said.

Trevor, "You were on that jury? I remember that trial."

Ahmed said, "And what was the verdict?" "He was…" Brad.

Trevor, "…guilty. Even though the old man was like 90 years old and had hearing and visual impairments, and the only reason he had a gun was that his home had been robbed like four times in one year."

"Six. Yeah, six." Brad. Trevor looked at Brad.

"And you all still convicted him."

He replied, "Yeah, he did it. He even said it on the stand. He was scared the guy was coming into his house and he knew he wouldn't be able to defend himself, so he shot through the door."

Jesse said, "So he admitted to being afraid for his life and that didn't carry any weight with the jury?"

Brad said, "Every legal gun owner knows that you don't fire until your life is in imminent danger. And you definitely don't just fire blindly through a door. What if the guy would have had a kid with him?"

Trevor says, "At three in the morning?" Brad said, "I said, "what if"."

Ahmed says, "May I ask you a question please?" Brad barely nodded and waited.

Ahmed, "Was this man, the shooter, a person of colour or a white man? Brad hesitates. He looks and sees them waiting for his response."

"Does it matter?" Brad asked.

Trevor said, "He was Mexican. And I'll give you one guess what the other guy was."

Jesse shook his head and turned his back to Brad.

Brad said, "Again with the race baiting. What difference does any of that make? He shot a guy."

Trevor said, "It establishes a pattern in your um...decision making."

"Yeah, it shows that I believe in the law and justice." Brad.

Trevor, "Uh huh. Making America great again, one guilty verdict at a time."

"But the man did shoot someone. Shouldn't he be punished? Why must you make it always about black and white?" Soo Lee said.

"I'm not the one making it about black versus white," Trevor says.

He slyly looked in Brad's direction.

"Historically it's been the faction with all of the power that causes division along racial lines. The oppressed don't have the power nor ability to manage that." Trevor says.

Brad, "Like I said earlier, there's always another option."

Trevor, "That's your way of saying, go back where I came from, right?"

Brad said, "Just saying."

Charles Hood was standing in front of the window as he was watching the people outside go about their lives.

Charles says, "You know, you can look out this window and see all those people walking around, black, white, brown, all the other colours, just living life, looking like we're just one big happy family. If you didn't know better you'd think we were the perfect little melting pot society."

Ahmed, "That was the goal of this country's forefathers, was it not?"

Trevor says, "Depends on who you ask."

Charles, "I don't know, was it? I'm the fourth generation of Hoods born in this country and we ain't never felt like we were part of the plan."

Brad, "That's because you're always complaining about what's wrong with this country instead of contributing to making it better."

Charles slowly turned to look Brad in the eye.

Charles was agitated.

"Contributing to make it better? Son, my great great grandfather was one of the slaves that helped build the white house in 1792. What was your great-grandfather doing? My grandson was killed in Iraq after 9/11, fighting for his country. Where were you? At home playing video games?"

Charles got emotional and his eyes filled with tears.

His 90-year-old legs begin to tremble.

"So don't you talk to me about contributing to this country? My family has contributed enough to this place and ain't never even got so much as a goddamn thank you!" Charles says.

He lost his balance and stumbled backwards. Brad and Trevor were first to rush to his side and caught him before he hit the floor. They each held him gently by the arm.

Trevor said, "Take it easy Unc."

Emily and Mercedes came to help Charles back to his seat.

Charles, "I'm sorry. Didn't mean to get worked up Mr. Foreman."

David said, "It's okay. But we should get back to talking about the case everyone."

CHAPTER 7

After a while, Deputy Stewart and Deputy Johnson were sitting in their chairs with their body language exposing the tension between them. Deputy Johnson's eyes were locked in a stare straight ahead down the empty hallway. Deputy Stewart had his eyes trained on a Guns and Ammo magazine. He abruptly closed the magazine and looked up.

Stewart said, "So let me ask you a question."

Deputy Johnson looked at him but didn't say anything.

Stewart said, "What if it was Joanie?"

Deputy Johnson gave Deputy Stewart his full attention now.

Johnson says, "What if what was Joanie?"

"This case. What if Joanie found herself in this situation and..."

"I've taught my daughter everything she needs to know about defending herself and getting out of those kinds of situations."

Stewart says, "Fair enough. But what if she didn't? Just for argument's sake. She didn't. And it was her word against the guy's word."

"What are you asking me, Stew?"

He sighed for a moment, then replied.

"I'm asking if you'd be so adamant that this kid was innocent if it was your daughter. That girl, York, she's someone's daughter man, and you...you and some of those people in that room are just dismissing her like she's some crazy chick calling the cops on a black guy in the park." Stewart said.

Johnson nodded.

"What you and a lot of other people need to understand, is that when you're a black man in THIS country, having a white woman call the cops on you for asking you to pick up your dog's crap, is the same as falsely accusing us of rape."

Stewart, "Oh come on A.J., how can you compare the two?"

Johnson said, "Because either one can ruin a black man's life. Or worse, end it."

"One crazy Karen shouldn't be an indictment on an entire race. Just like one gangbanger or drug dealer is an indictment on an entire race."

"Yeah well if that were the case we'd probably be unemployed."

"Well?"

Johnson said, "Well what?"

Stewart said, "Answer the question. What if it was Joanie?"

"If it was my daughter, I'd be the one on trial…" Johnson.

"Right. Regardless of physical evidence there was or wasn't. Regardless of the race of the offender. Right?" Stewart said.

"She's my daughter. This is different. I'm not involved so I can look at the situation objectively without any biases or prejudices."

"Really? Can you?"

Back inside the Jury room, most of the jurors were back at the table. Brad was sitting on the large window silicone side of the room and Jesse was sitting on the floor with his back against the wall.

Ahmed said, "What about injuries or wounds?"

Emily said, "We already talked about that. She didn't have any, remember."

Ahmed, "No, not the young lady. The young man. If it was an attack, shouldn't she have tried to defend herself which would have resulted in some kind of injury."

Sanayah said, "A scratch or cut maybe. Something." Emily says, "There wasn't anything."

David said, "I doubt there'd be anything like that after four weeks anyway."

Trevor said, "Oh well…"

Soo Lee asked, "Does that make you happy?"

Trevor, "You know what? It does. Because if this really happened, which it didn't, and she waited so long to report it that all of the evidence is gone, then score one for us. For a change."

Mercedes said, "You're sick."

"I'm real. The rules in this country aren't designed to be fair. So we gotta take a win wherever we can get it.'?" Trevor said.

Mercedes, "A win?" Brad, "Like O.J.?" Trevor says, "Exactly."

Mercedes shook her head again in disgust.

Trevor said, "I didn't make these rules. I'm just forced to play by them. Besides, all of that is moot, because he didn't rape her."

Mercedes looked at Emily.

"How do any verdicts get made like this? It's impossible."

Emily, "It may seem that way but the system does work."

Trevor chuckled.

Sanayah, "Yes, the system does work. It's what makes America so great."

Trevor says, "Jesus Christ."

Brad, "You got a problem with her saying that?"

Trevor says, "I thought that was obvious." Brad pointed at the door.

Brad, "There's the door."

Trevor says, "You don't think I would if I could. Once you're born here, you're trapped. It's damn near impossible to just pack up and leave."

Soo Lee says, "Why would you want to? Where else would you go better than America?"

Trevor said, "Trust me, there are alternatives.

Especially for people that look like us."

He pointed to Gladys, Charles and Jesse but ignored Mercedes.

Trevor said, "Black people need to just go somewhere that isn't always reminding us that we're not wanted."

Sanayah said, "America is home to all people.

Everyone is welcome. Don't you believe that?"

Gladys says, "Sometimes you have to look at peoples,' or in this case, a country's actions instead of the words that are written on centuries-old documents honey."

Jesse says, "Immigrants like you and your family, come here and get better opportunities, better treatment than black families that have been here since the beginning."

Trevor said, "The weight of that oppression over so many years can break a people."

David says, "But what about what black people do to themselves?"

Brad said, "Thank you!"

David, "There's a lot that's wrong with the black community that has nothing to do with racism or America. It's how you treat yourselves, it's the things you prioritize. Immigrants like her dad come here and take advantage of all of the opportunities this country has to offer. He worked hard, he saved money and he built a business."

Trevor, "Her father didn't come here with a bullseye on his back either."

Brad, "Here we go with the public enemy number one theory. How about maybe you're your own worst enemy."

David, "That's not what I'm saying."

"Well, it's what I'm saying," Brad says.

"Do you two even know how racist you sound right now? The fact that you can't even acknowledge how deeply systemic racism has infected the roots of this country. I mean, how could it not, the country was built on white people taking advantage of and oppressing people of colour. Any colour, pick one! But one thing always remains the same, the oppressor. Flip through the pages of any history book and you'll see just how long Europeans have been subjugating indigenous, black and brown people. The sooner we can get out of here the better and let's see how they do here without us." Trevor said.

The room was quiet for a brief moment. Then Jorge broke the silence.

Jorge, "Si', I agree. The sooner we get out of this room, the better."

There was a pause and then there was a short burst of soft laughter from everyone. Then in an instant, the room was quiet again.

Emily, "I hate to say this but I don't think we're going to be able to reach a verdict."

There were a few moans and grumblings.

Emily said, "We're just too far apart and divided in what we feel. We all heard the same things in the courtroom but our interpretations of those things are all over the place."

Sanayah said, "But then we will be allowing rapists to go free."

Jesse, "Or we'd be allowing a liar to ruin a man's life.

And for what? So her daddy won't be mad at her?" Mercedes, "So what do we do?"

David said, "We take another vote."

Everyone whined and moaned their disapproval again.

David, "But this time we vote on whether to tell the judge we can't come to a decision."

Emily said, "A hung jury?" David says, "Right."

Emily said, "Is everyone clear on what that means?"

Brad said, "It means woke ism strikes again." Trevor glares in Brad's direction.

Soo Lee says, "It means everybody wins." Charles says, "No darling, it means nobody wins."

CHAPTER 8

Back to the outside of the Jury room, Deputy Stewart was sitting in his chair on his cell phone. Deputy Johnson was standing up as he was leaning against the wall, still gazing down the empty hallway.

Stewart, "It got awfully quiet in there."

Johnson thought something for a moment, then he said.

"Maybe they finally figured out how to communicate respectfully."

Stewart looked at him before saying, "Or maybe they fell asleep.."

Both men laughed until Deputy Johnson's phone rang. He checked the caller ID. He puts his finger to his mouth to gesture for Deputy Stewart to be quiet. Then he answered.

Johnson says, "Hello Judge." He listened from the other side.

"Uh, no not yet. They've been in there hammering away at it though."

Deputy Stewart watched as Deputy Johnson's facial expression changed as he listened.

Johnson, "I...I'm sorry your honour..."

Stewart was getting more confused as well as a bit concerned.

"What did you just say?"

A look of concern came over the face of Johnson and Deputy Stewart noticed it and stood up.

Stewart whispered, "What? What happened?" Deputy Johnson held up his finger.

Johnson said, "Uh yes, I understand your honour.

Yes, ma'am."

Johnson was listening to the other side reply very carefully.

"I understood, right away. Thanks for letting us know." He said.

Johnson nodded in agreement.

"I'll relay your appreciation. Take care." He ended the call.

Stewart said, "What was that all about?"

Deputy Johnson put his phone away, then lowered his head and let out a loud exhale.

A few moments later, the jurors were in smaller groups talking quietly amongst themselves. Jorge was standing alone looking out the window. He saw a lot of commotion outside. News vans were pulling up to the courthouse.

Jorge said, "Hey, something's going on out there."

Everyone made their way over to a window. They saw the commotion outside.

Gladys said, "Should we be worried? Could it be a bomb threat or something?"

David shook his head immediately.

David, "No, if it was a bomb threat everybody would be running out of the building instead of in…"

Emily said, "Something big must have happened in one of the other trials that's going on."

Suddenly there was a loud knock on the door. It scared some of them. The door opened and Deputy Johnson and Deputy Stewart walked in with sombre faces. Deputy Johnson was carrying a small black duffel bag.

Trevor said, "Hey, what's going on out there?"

Charles said, "Something we should know."

Johnson looked around the room filled with concerned faces.

Johnson, "Actually, yes."

He had everyone's full attention as they were waiting anxiously for his next words.

Johnson said, "Were you able to agree on a verdict?"

They all looked around at one another as they were all embarrassed.

Trevor said, "Tell him Mr. Foreman."

David said, "Well, unfortunately, no. The only thing we could all agree on is that we can't agree on anything about this case."

David looked at everyone's face.

"There are just too many differences of opinion." Then, Johnson sighed for a moment and said.

"Well, that's what we came in here to tell you. The judge wanted to relay her appreciation for you all carrying out your civic duty to the best of your ability, but you can stop deliberations now."

Trevor said, "Don't tell me the kid took a plea deal…"

Johnson shook his head looking at him. "No…"

Emily said, "Were the charges dropped?" Johnson, "No."

Charles, "Well what happened son? We've been in this room all day, not to mention sitting in that courtroom for three weeks."

Trevor and Mercedes looked at each other for a moment. Then at Johnson.

"Why the sudden cease and desist?" Charles asked.

Deputy Johnson cleared his throat and hesitated to speak. While he tried to come up with the right words, Deputy Stewart stepped in front of the group.

Stewart said, "Myron Peterson hung himself an hour ago."

Emily said, "What? Gladys, "Dear God."

This made everyone shocked. Some were distraught. Gladys, Emily and Sanayah began to cry. Brad shook his head and Trevor paced in circles, angrily with his hands over his head.

Jesse, "If we could have just…"

Johnson stopped him immediately saying.

"There was nothing you could do. This is not on you or anyone else except Mr. Peterson. This was his decision."

Charles's voice revealed his pain.

"Because we couldn't make one…" He said.

Johnson looked at all those disappointed faces as he sighed as say.

"Listen to me, all of you."

Slowly, many heads went up to look at him.

"You did your civic duty and you did it to the best of your ability. That's it. You are not going to be held accountable for his actions."

Everyone listened to him carefully and some of them nodded as they agreed with him.

"You can all go home knowing that you did everything that was asked of you."

Jesse shook his head once again. "It doesn't feel like that."

There was a moment of silence in the room. Then Deputy Johnson opened the black bag and reached into it.

Johnson said, "I have all of your personal belongings."

He started to hand out wallets and cell phones. He pulled out a phone and held it up.

Trevor said, "That's me…"

He held out his hands from the other side of the room as he was signalling for the Deputy to toss it.

Johnson asked, "You sure?" Trevor nodded.

"I got it."

The deputy tossed the phone into the air. Trevor tried to catch it with one hand but it bounced out of his hand.

He tried to catch it with his other hand but missed and it hit the floor. When it hit the floor, the phone came on. The screensaver lightened up. It was a photo of Trevor and a white woman as they were smiling. He picked it up and unlocked the phone but not before Brad peeked over and saw the picture.

Brad said, "Well I'll be damned…" Everyone stopped.

Brad, "You mean to tell me that all this time, despite all your rhetoric about white devils and Karens, you got jungle fever."

The room was silent and all eyes were on Trevor. He quickly swiped the photo off the screen and turned the phone off.

Trevor said, "No, you ass. That's my mother…" Brad was stunned.

"Your mother?!"

Trevor didn't say anything. But that was enough for Brad.

"Well, that's even better."

Mercedes, "Wait a minute, you mean you're biracial?"

Trevor asked, "And?"

Mercedes smiled and shook her head. Mercedes, "Nothing."

The deputies continued passing out belongings and one by one the jurors left the room until there were just Deputy Johnson and Deputy Stewart.

Johnson, "Sometimes I really hate this job." Stewart smiled.

"It's like you told them. This isn't on you. That kid did what he did to get himself in trouble and then was too afraid to face up to the consequences."

"You still believe that?"

"You still don't? Why else would he take the coward's way out?"

Johnson thought something for a moment. "Maybe he thought his life had been ruined." Stewart looked at him.

"Maybe he felt like just the accusation and stigma would follow him around for the rest of his life and he didn't know how to handle that."

They looked at each other, and then around the room. Stewart said, "Guess we'll never know."

Deputy Stewart walked out of the room. Deputy Johnson took a moment before turning off the light and leaving

CHAPTER 9

A few days later under the vibrant canopy of the Korean market in South Central Los Angeles, the energy buzzed like electricity through the air. Amongst the colourful storefronts and tantalizing aromas, Sarah and Michael found themselves standing outside a bustling grocery store, its doors invitingly open. Sarah's eyes sparkled with anticipation as she gazed at the array of exotic produce displayed just beyond the entrance.

"I can't wait to explore this place, Michael. I've heard they have the best kimchi in town!"

Michael grinned, the excitement evident in his voice.

"I'm looking forward to trying some new flavours.

Let's dive in!"

As they stepped closer to the store, the scent of spices and fresh vegetables enveloped them like a warm embrace. Sarah paused, inhaling deeply as she savoured the familiar tang of sesame and soy.

"Isn't it amazing how a single smell can transport you to a different world?" she mused, her eyes alight with wonder.

Michael nodded in agreement, his senses alive with the sights and sounds of Koreatown.

"It's like we're on a culinary adventure, discovering new tastes and experiences with every step."

Just then, a group of teenagers burst out of the store, their laughter echoing through the bustling street. They clutched bags filled with snacks and drinks, their faces flushed with excitement. Sarah watched them with a wistful smile, her mind drifting back to her own teenage years spent exploring the vibrant streets of Los Angeles.

"Remember when we used to roam these streets for hours, Michael? It feels like a lifetime ago."

Michael chuckled, a nostalgic twinkle in his eye.

"Those were the days, Sarah. But hey, who says we can't still have a little fun?"

With a playful grin, he took her hand and led her through the open doorway of the store, their laughter mingling with the sounds of the bustling market.

Inside, the aisles were alive with activity as shoppers browsed the shelves, their carts filled with a colourful array of groceries. The sound of Korean pop music filled the air, adding to the lively atmosphere. Sarah's eyes widened with delight as she took in the sights and sounds of the bustling store.

"It's like stepping into a different world," she whispered, her voice filled with awe.

Michael nodded, his own excitement mounting as he scanned the shelves for familiar favourites.

"There's so much to see and taste here. Where do we even start?"

They wandered through the aisles, their senses overwhelmed by the tantalizing array of flavours and aromas. From savoury bulgogi to sweet rice cakes, the store was a treasure trove of culinary delights. As they reached the produce section, Sarah's eyes lit up with excitement as she spotted a display of bright red chilli peppers.

"I've always wanted to try making kimchi at home.

Do you think we should give it a try?"

Michael grinned, his stomach growling at the thought of the spicy fermented cabbage dish.

"Why not? I'm always up for a culinary adventure!"

With their basket filled to the brim with exotic ingredients, Sarah and Michael made their way to the checkout counter, their hearts full of anticipation for the culinary delights that awaited them. As they stepped back out into the bustling streets of Koreatown, they knew that their taste buds were in for a treat.

Soo Lee was working in her father's store. There was a television on the wall and it was showing a Breaking News report. Soo Lee stopped what she was doing when she recognized the woman on the screen. It was Amanda York. The scrolling ticker read "Woman Arrested After Confessing False Rape Accusation". Soo Lee covered her mouth in shock.

Inside the common room, Charles Hood was sitting on a couch with another elderly man. They were watching the news report also.

Charles says, "Dammit."

Mercedes was walking on campus scrolling through her phone when the report about Amanda York popped up on her phone. Mercedes stopped walking and looked around confused. She covered her face with her hand.

Jorge was sitting on his front porch watching several gang members across the street who were standing around a car playing loud music. He got a notification on his phone. He looked at it and saw Amanda York's name.

Brad was sitting behind a desk in a suit. He was on the internet and saw the Amanda York story on a news website.

Brad said, "Shoulda kept your mouth shut."

He shook his head and clicked on a new website.

On the other side, Glady was in her bedroom as she was sitting on the edge of the bed watching the breaking news and crying.

Trevor was sitting in his car which was parked in a parking lot. He was reading the news about Amanda. His eyes fill with tears. His hand gripped the steering wheel and squeezed.

At last Amanda York was being escorted into the courthouse in handcuffs by Deputy Stewart and Deputy Johnson. They looked at each other with stoic expressions.

Stewart, "Can't say anything man..." Johnson smiled a bit looking at him.

"It will be better for you..." He replied.

A group of media people were close to them. As they were questioning and trying to get a glimpse of Amanda

York. But both the deputies led her away from the reporters into the building. Finally, the door slowly closed behind them.

EPILOGUE

The early morning sun cast a golden glow over the quiet streets as James hurried along his usual route to the courthouse. He glanced at his watch, cursing under his breath as he realized he was running late. As a public defender, punctuality was essential, but today seemed determined to thwart his efforts.

Just as he rounded the corner, James spotted a figure huddled against the wall of a rundown building. Curiosity tugged at him, prompting him to approach. As he drew nearer, he saw that it was a young man, his clothes dishevelled and his face etched with worry.

"Hey, are you okay?" James asked, his voice laced with concern.

The young man looked up, his eyes wide with desperation.

"I...I don't know," he stammered, his voice trembling. "I'm in some trouble."

James crouched down beside him, his brow furrowing with concern.

"What kind of trouble?" he asked gently.

The young man hesitated for a moment before blurting out, "I've been accused of something I didn't do."

James was confused.

"They're saying I raped someone."

James was stunned but felt a pang of sympathy for the young man. He knew all too well the devastating impact of false accusations, having witnessed countless trials where lives were shattered by unfounded claims.

"Take a deep breath," James said, his voice soothing. "We'll figure this out together."

As they sat together on the sidewalk, James listened intently as the young man poured out his story. He spoke of a nightmarish encounter with the police, of being dragged from his home in the dead of night and thrown into a cell like a common criminal.

"It's like they've already made up their minds," the young man said, his voice thick with despair.

James shook his head.

"They don't care about the truth, only about closing another case."

James nodded sympathetically, his heart aching for the injustice the young man had endured.

"Unfortunately, that's all too common," he said, his voice tinged with bitterness.

The young man looked at him.

James sighed and added, "Especially in cases like this, where the stigma of rape clouds judgment and distorts perceptions."

The young man nodded, his eyes brimming with tears.

"But what can I do?" he asked, his voice pleading. "How can I prove my innocence when everyone already sees me as guilty?"

James placed a reassuring hand on the young man's shoulder.

"We'll start by gathering evidence," he said, his voice firm.

"How?"

"We'll track down witnesses, review surveillance footage, anything that can help build your case."

As they spoke, James couldn't shake the sinking feeling in the pit of his stomach. Rape cases were on the rise, the courts were inundated with harrowing tales of violence and violation. But amidst the grim statistics and legal complexities, he refused to lose sight of the human beings at the heart of each case, both accuser and accused alike.

"The truth will come to light," James said, his voice filled with conviction. "And when it does, justice will prevail."

The young man nodded, a glimmer of hope flickering in his eyes.

"Thank you," he said, his voice choked with emotion. He thought something for a moment then said.

"I don't know what I would've done without your help."

James smiled warmly, a sense of purpose coursing through his veins.

"You're not alone in this," he said, his voice unwavering.

"I'll be with you…"

"Really?"

"Yeah… We'll fight this together, every step of the way."

As they rose to their feet, James felt a renewed sense of determination wash over him. He may have been late for work, but at that moment, he knew that he was exactly where he needed to be. For in a world plagued by injustice and inequality, it was up to people like him to stand up for what was right, to be a voice for the voiceless, and to ensure that justice was served, no matter the cost.

The city stirred to life around them as James and the young man continued their conversation, their voices rising above the din of traffic and the chatter of passersby. They moved to a nearby bench, finding solace in the quiet sanctuary of a small park nestled amidst the urban sprawl. As they sat, James listened intently as the young man shared more details of his ordeal. He spoke of the fear and humiliation he had felt at the hands of the police, of the accusatory glances and whispered rumours that had followed him since the allegations were made.

"It's like my whole life has been turned upside down," the young man said, his voice heavy with despair.

"I can't sleep, I can't eat…I feel like I'm drowning in a sea of uncertainty."

James nodded sympathetically, his heart aching for the young man's anguish. He knew all too well the toll that false accusations could take on a person's mental and emotional well-being, the relentless pressure to prove one's innocence in the face of overwhelming scepticism.

"You're not alone in feeling that way," James said, his voice gentle but resolute. "But you have to remember that you're stronger than you think. You have the right to be heard, to defend yourself against these accusations."

The young man nodded, his gaze fixed on the ground beneath his feet.

"I just don't know if I have the strength to keep fighting," he admitted, his voice barely above a whisper.

James reached out and placed a reassuring hand on the young man's shoulder.

"You do," he said, his voice firm. "And you have people who believe in you, who are willing to stand by your side no matter what."

As they sat together in silence, James felt a sense of kinship with the young man beside him. Despite the vast differences in their backgrounds and experiences, they were bound together by a shared sense of injustice, and a shared determination to seek truth and uphold justice.

"The system may be flawed," James said, breaking the silence that had settled between them.

The young man nodded.

"But that doesn't mean we can't fight to change it. We can't let ourselves be defeated by the very institutions that are meant to protect us."

The young man looked up, his eyes meeting James with a newfound sense of resolve.

"You're right," he said, his voice stronger now. "I won't let this destroy me. I'll keep fighting until my name is cleared until justice is served."

James smiled, a flicker of pride swelling in his chest.

"That's the spirit," he said, his voice filled with admiration. "And I'll be right there beside you every step of the way."

As they rose to their feet, James felt a renewed sense of purpose coursing through his veins. He may have been late for work, but at that moment, he knew that he was exactly where he needed to be. For in a world plagued by injustice and inequality, it was up to people like him to stand up for what was right, to be a voice for the voiceless, and to ensure that justice was served, no matter the cost. And with the young man by his side, he knew that they could face whatever challenges lay ahead, together.

THE END